Chapter 1:

The Wooers that Dance

Tim was having a miserable time at the nightclub tonight. From the bar Tim watched those nightclubbers dancing on the dance floor. The flashing lights blinding. The deafening music blaring out loud. Every track was playing dance music.

Tim hated it here. He wanted to leave the nightclub now. His friend Terry seemed to be having a good time. Terry took pleasure from his hedonistic excitement. He flirted with a flirtatious woman. The Hedonist was gratified from pleasure, desiring to be seduced. Standing and watching Tim took an interest in the female nightclubbers dancing. Earlier he made no impression on any of them. The women undesired him. Naturally of course. The uninterested women took no notice of him. The female nightclubbers were uninterested in the unappealing and undesirable men. The surrounding women dancing took no interest in a man dancing. The man's chest was revealed from his unbuttoned shirt and hanging from his neck was a gold medallion.

The excited women danced next to him. Admiring the good-looking man dancing. The stranger made such an admirable impression from his good dance moves. He danced well.

Watching and losing interest in them, Tim frowned and sulked. He seemed deeply unhappy and miserable. He hadn't spoken at all.

Terry came up to Tim who stood watching them.

"Aren't you going to dance?" asked Terry.

"No, I am not dancing. Why don't you dance? Go ahead. You dance without me," replied Tim.

"C'mon, buddy. Dance," encouraged Terry.

In a bad mood, Tim felt unhappy.

"No. You dance. Why did I come? I am having a bloody awful time."

"C'mon dance!" insisted Terry.

Tim felt sorry for himself. He regretted going to the nightclub.

"I really shouldn't have come. What did I come for?"

"You're here now. So don't make it any worse for yourself. Why don't you dance?" suggested Terry.

Tim still had an inhibition. He had no wish to dance. He remained unenthusiastic about dancing. He still regretted coming to the nightclub tonight. He was feeling sad, miserable and vulnerable. Amongst all these nightclubbers and ravers present. Was this seemingly going to be the worst day of Tim's life?

Feeling moody, unenthusiastic and unexcited, Tim preferred not to dance.

"Go on! You go and dance," gestured Tim.

Terry had the enthusiasm to dance now. His interest to dance a keenness. Terry walked away by going to a dance floor with flashing lights. There Terry danced on the dance floor. Terry was good at dancing. Alone by himself, Tim went to a bar where there he bought a beer for himself. Perspiring and feeling thirsty, he gulped it down. Quenching his thirst. He soon lost his inhibitions. He became less self-conscious.

There sitting in a seating area the women talked. They had stayed together in their groups. Some of them were rather attractive and prettier. The women sat at tables and engaged in conversation. A few others joined in the conversation. Two of them were professional secretaries and the other one a professional beautician and the last but not least a model.

Tim took a glance at them. He desired them. One of them was a stunner. He envied them. They attracted far more attention. The shy, quieter woman dressed in a black dress wearing a necklace, bracelets, bangles and sleepers was much sexier and lovelier than them. The chatty others intended to have a girls' night out. They wore lacy lingerie.

Tim desired the buxom blonde dressed in black. Her sexy figure was curvaceous thus revealing the cleavage of her beautiful breasts under the cups of her lacy black bra. Tim fantasised about the blonde he desired. Desiring her beauty. He was smitten at the sight of her. With his desire for her, he had been lost in his fantasy.

Suddenly, Terry came back to the bar. He disturbed Tim who was lost in a daydream. He had been daydreaming. Terry stood in front of Tim. With his hands, he distracted him in front of Tim's face. Tim's expression was sad and childish.

"C'mon. Let's dance," suggested Terry.

Losing interest in the blue-eyed beauty. He thought the blonde was a tantalizer and a bore! Tim was titillated by the sight of the provocative women. Tim lost his desire for the tantalizer. Tim got up and stretched out his legs. Tim found Terry and they both went to the crowded dance floor where they both found space to dance. They danced with strangers, nightclubbers and ravers.

Suddenly a voluptuous brunette appeared. Tim marvelled at her beauty. The brunette's voluptuousness was irresistible. The brunette danced well. Attracting attention. The beautiful brunette had been surrounded by women dancing. The brunette dancing preferred Tim, not Terry.

Tim danced next to her, smelling her perspiration and the fine scent of her beautiful perfume. Her long hair was flying in the air.

Tim desired her. Tim drooled and swooned at the gorgeous woman. Tim felt a deep love for her. The brunette dancing gracefully attracted him. She was the centre of attraction.

The woman perspired. Her complexion was ruddy. Her cheeks rosier from being flushed. Tim smelled the scent of her perfume as well as the woman's perspiration. Tim felt enamoured and enraptured. He desired and loved her.

The woman's beautiful eyes glinted with brilliance. Both wooers wooed each other while dancing. They both were overwhelmed with such deep love. Their desire for each other was captivating.

From the sound and playing of this dance track. This dance remained short. The music changed and another dance track played.

Suddenly within moments, the brunette vanished. She vanished out of sight.

Tim was very sad when the brunette had gone. Tim was deeply disappointed when he lost sight of her. Probably Tim would never see her ever again!

Feeling deeply sad Tim left the crowded dance floor with Terry joining him.

Late at night, they both left the crowded nightclub. They both walked to a parked car down the road. They both got in a banger. Terry drove off. Driving his friend Tim back to his house.

Chapter 2:
Tim Spent Time with his Brother and Wife

Tim stayed at his brother's house. His elder brother Stewart is happily married to Clara his wife.

In the luxurious lounge, they all had tea together. They sat in front of the fireplace where they were more comfortable. There they warmed up. Indulging in the comfort of luxury. They luxuriated in the luxury suite. The firelight flickered in the dark and shadows. In a corner, there was a lampstand from which a lamp shone in the shadowy dark lounge.

Tim sipped his tea. Relaxing in luxuriousness. Enjoying the comfort. He wasn't talkative.

"How is work?" asked Clara.

"It's fine. It's a family business. I have lots of things to do," replied Tim.

With curious wonder, Stewart's wife enquired,

"How is the painting?" asked Clara.

"It's good. I am getting on with it fine."

"Any good ones?" asked Clara.

desired and loved her.

The woman's beautiful eyes glinted with brilliance. Both wooers wooed each other while dancing. They both were overwhelmed with such deep love. Their desire for each other was captivating.

From the sound and playing of this dance track. This dance remained short. The music changed and another dance track played.

Suddenly within moments, the brunette vanished. She vanished out of sight.

Tim was very sad when the brunette had gone. Tim was deeply disappointed when he lost sight of her. Probably Tim would never see her ever again!

Feeling deeply sad Tim left the crowded dance floor with Terry joining him.

Late at night, they both left the crowded nightclub. They both walked to a parked car down the road. They both got in a banger. Terry drove off. Driving his friend Tim back to his house.

Chapter 2:
Tim Spent Time with his Brother and Wife

Tim stayed at his brother's house. His elder brother Stewart is happily married to Clara his wife.

In the luxurious lounge, they all had tea together. They sat in front of the fireplace where they were more comfortable. There they warmed up. Indulging in the comfort of luxury. They luxuriated in the luxury suite. The firelight flickered in the dark and shadows. In a corner, there was a lampstand from which a lamp shone in the shadowy dark lounge.

Tim sipped his tea. Relaxing in luxuriousness. Enjoying the comfort. He wasn't talkative.

"How is work?" asked Clara.

"It's fine. It's a family business. I have lots of things to do," replied Tim.

With curious wonder, Stewart's wife enquired,

"How is the painting?" asked Clara.

"It's good. I am getting on with it fine."

"Any good ones?" asked Clara.

Tim preferred not to brag about things.

"I paint different things. According to the subject matter."

"What are you painting now?" enquired Clara.

"I have done a still life. I have painted various things," answered Tim.

"You should paint me," suggested Clara.

Tim leaned forward. He took a closer look at Clara sitting. Clara was a handsome married woman.

"Paint you? Do you really want me to paint you? I could paint you. If you want me to."

"Oh! Yes. I insist. You can do it. Can you?"

With enthusiasm, Tim showed an eager interest in painting Clara.

"I would love to paint you. It shouldn't be a problem," said Tim enthusiastically.

The Husband ogled his emotional wife.

"Tim, please paint my wife. Oh! Please. It would please me."

"Yes. I would like to. It will be a pleasure," grinned Tim.

"Can you do it?" asked Stewart.

"Yes. I can do it," assured his Brother.

Tim looked closely at his Brother's wife. Clara's curly long hair with ringlets and her good looks.

"One night I saw a dream woman. I would have loved to have painted her. Why am I saying this? Painting you would be another experience. Quite interesting," blabbed Tim.

Clara clasp her hands together.

"You will paint me. I take that as a yes," smiled Clara.

"Of course, I will. I give you my word," assured Tim.

"Good! Who is this woman you saw?" asked Clara.

"I rather not say. You see a face! Yes, I must paint that," blurted out Tim.

"When can you do it?" asked Brother.

"I am busy. I will let you know," responded Tim.

"Oh! Please do. I can't wait for you to paint my wife. It will be pleasing."

Tim agreed to paint Clara.

"I will paint your wife."

"Tim. You should get married," said Brother.

Tim was disillusioned with marriage.

"I don't know. I don't think I will. I am too happy holding onto my dreams. Dreaming."

"You're a dreamer," remarked Brother.

"Once I start painting, I am lost in deep concentration. I am lost in another world. The Artist's world," admitted Tim.

"You're a good painter," remarked Clara.

Tim expressed his aestheticism.

"Creativity is good. Depending on the matter."

On a table, Tim saw a beautiful wedding photograph of a Husband and Wife. His handsome Brother with his handsome Wife. It inspired him. It gave him some initiative to paint his Brother's wife. His Brother naturally loved and adored his wife. Soon it will be their Wedding Anniversary. In preparation for their Wedding Anniversary celebration.

Tim would be delighted to paint his Brother's lovely wife. He wanted to start right away on it. With an obligation as a favour to his Brother. Painting is a passion of his. An obsession. He has an aesthetic obsessiveness for the Arts.

Agreeing to paint Clara. Tim assured them with his motivational intention.

"Give me time. I will start it early next month," confirmed Tim.

"That's fine by us. Please do," acknowledged Wife.

Leaving Husband and Wife together. The married couple indulged in a nightcap. Tim went upstairs to a spare bedroom where there he stayed the night.

On previous days his Brother had been neglectful to him in spending that time with his beloved wife. A truly romantic relationship between them. He thought of getting married. Marriage in the future now seemed quite unlikely. It was an unrealistic fantasy. Tim dreamt of marriage. He had wonderful dreams of it. In his mind he visualised marriage. He pictured it. The prospects of marriage. The marriage perspective. What were his ideals of marriage? He had unfulfilling expectations of marriage. Of course marriage itself was wonderful!

Tim romanticised having a romance. He had fantasies of being married. His marriage fantasies were truly wonderful. The romance was exciting.

Chapter 3:
The Artist's Favourite Portrait

One rainy afternoon a Model arrived at the studio. Tim, an Artist, greeted the young woman. The voluptuous model took off her raincoat. She revealed her beautiful figure. The model wore a toga. Tim led the model down the studio. Stopping at the exact spot. He positioned the model to a spot where the curvaceous model stood still and beautifully posed in a position. She was the image of an Athenian, Grecian posing. Her exposed cleavage was revealed. The sight of her breasts was beautiful.

Standing at the easel the Artist began to paint the image of the Grecian, Greek standing and posing naturally. Her countenance was radiant as well as nonchalant too. She had an expression of nonchalance in her pose.

Standing still the Athenian posed at an angle with such grace. The light was shining and reflecting. Her cheeks glowed. Her complexion was fresh.

Using a paintbrush the Artist painted using oil paints on a canvas. After hours of posing for the Artist, the model grew tired of standing still and posing. When the Artist had ended his first session of painting the Grecian, he then told her she could leave. He reminded her that she had to come back tomorrow at midday.

Tim felt exhausted from painting. He rested for the rest of the day. With discipline and commitment, he prepared himself for painting tomorrow.

The following day the painter resume his painting. At noon the Artist started the next session. He continued doing his painting. Today he finished off the portrait. The Artist marvelled at his work. Desiring the gorgeous model. He did revere her. Having the utmost respect and high regard for her. He paid the model her fee and thanked her. Wishing to use her again in the near future. He ended up hanging the portrait on the wall in the studio. Standing still he admired it. He became too proud of it. He marvelled at the Greek imagery of it. The Grecian image of the Athenian posing.

The same model posing yesterday and today was exceptional and extraordinary. She was truly a professional model. A Godsend! With pride, he professed himself as an Artist to the model. She seemed impressed by the impressive Artist.

Standing and looking at a portrait hanging on the wall. In the light. Tim marvelled at it and admired it. He painted a good portrait. He considered it to be a great one.

With satisfaction from painting it. He had immense joy. He would never be able to do something comparable to this ever again!

Before walking away. He admired it again. By looking at his favourite portrait for a short while with such joyful admiration.

Chapter 4:
Tim Paints his Brother's Wife

At noon the Artist welcomed Clara who came into the studio. Today was a sunny day. Tim giving instructions had gestured, pointing to the chair facing the easel. Clara sat down on the chair. In the background there was lighting. Clara wore a pretty floral patterned dress. She looked fashionably dressed. Clara had finely applied makeup. Her features were accentuated. Clara looked handsome. Clara took comfort from sitting. She kept still. Clara beautifully posed as the Artist painted. Her fine figure was desirably appealing. Clara had an appealing attraction. Her fairness was an attractiveness.

Tim took his time painting Clara. His painting was admirable and impressive. He beautifully painted Clara. With a sense of wonder, Clara wanted to know what the actual portrait looked like. To see it close up.

Wanting to get it done, Tim painted faster and faster. He wanted to finish the portrait sooner. He had no wish to spend another session on it. Clara sat with such patience while posing. Clara enjoyed the experience of being painted by an Artist. Clara had been calm, attentive and relaxed when sitting and posing. Her natural expression was joyful and happy.

Within a few hours, Tim had completed a portrait of

Clara.

The canvas on the easel. Standing together they both admired it.

"It's you," pointed Tim.

"That's me. It's lovely," remarked Clara.

Clara kissed Tim appreciatively. In appreciation, Clara hugged Tim. A passionate hug. Clara had an appreciation for his thoughtfulness.

Going home Clara rejoiced. Clara told her Husband about the lovely portrait.

The next day Tim had the portrait framed. Then followed by having the portrait bubble-wrapped.

Subsequently, Clara collected her portrait. In self-admiration Clara had self-love!

Clara was a very happy customer. Of course, it was a family favour. A good one. Out of obligation. It was a motivation of the Artist.

Going to his brother's house. Clara and her Husband and Tim stood together and looked at the portrait hanging on a wall in the Living Room. (A reproduction had been removed and taken down.)

They admired the portrait of Clara, his Brother's wife. They marvelled at the sight of it. Admiring it. What a marvellous modern portrait!

"Is that me?" said Wife.

"Yes, it's you," smiled Husband.

"Is it me?"

"It is you."

"It's lovely!" exclaimed Wife.

"You have made my day. Thank you, Tim. Thanks," said Brother appreciatively.

Tim and his Brother gloated over the portrait. Marvelling at it again.

"Yep! It's a good one!"

Chapter 5: Tim's Enjoyable Relaxation Indoors

That weekend Tim stayed at his Brother's house. Out in the garden, he spent time with his Brother and Wife. It was a beautiful summer. The garden looked lovely, in summertime a marvellous beauty.

With wonder, Tim admired the garden. Marvelling at the sight of the rose bushes with their beautiful roses. So immaculate were the budding rosebuds.

He smelled the rose scent in the air. Of the garden which was redolent of roses. Its pure fine exquisiteness of the scent of roses.

Tim sat on a garden chair out in the garden with his Brother and his daydreaming romantic wife. Clara looked restful and relaxed sitting in a graceful position.

"Will you get married?" asked Clara.

"Me? No, it's unlikely," answered Tim.

"Tim's single. Tim won't find anyone," laughed Brother.

Tim kept calm.

"I shan't find anyone. I won't get married. Marriage won't happen," said Tim miserably.

"Oh! That is a shame. Be positive. Be optimistic," said Clara.

Tim cooled down. "I am being realistic. It's becoming more unlikely."

"Don't you dream of it?" asked Clara.

"I do think of it. It's unrealistic," frowned Tim.

Tim felt uncomfortable sitting down for a long time. He ached from discomfort. He suffered from a slight cramp.

Going back indoors, Tim went to a hammock and lay down on it. Feeling comfort and being comfortable. In the silence, he rested on a hammock. Taking such comfort from lying down on it. Suspended at a high position attached to something. He did enjoy the comfort of lying down on the springy hammock. Tim did enjoy his rest. In solitude, it was quieter, cooler and shadier in there. With his privacy, he enjoyed his freedom and peace and quiet. From the open windows there, he felt invigorated by the fresh air. The air was cool. Its coolness from a light breeze. He cooled down in the cooler shade. Tim dozed off. There he rested in peace lying down on a hammock.

Chapter 6:
The Portrait (The Sitting)

Suddenly a landline rang. Tim entered an upstairs room to answer the telephone, an extension. He picked up the receiver and spoke. His voice was hoarse.

"Hello," answered Tim.

"It's me. Katrina. Please can you paint me?"

"Sure. I can do that. Meet me at the studio tomorrow at midday."

"That would be great. Thank you."

"What sort of thing do you want me to do?" asked Tim.

"Do me a portrait," insisted Katrina.

"What style? Is it old fashioned or a modern style one?"

"I'd like it to be modern if I can."

"Good! Then that's settled."

"Goodbye!" said Katrina sweetly.

"Goodbye!"

Tim put the telephone down. Tim felt buoyed up. He was pleased with himself at having made an appointment. He looked forward to meeting Katrina tomorrow at noon. Tim desired and fancied Katrina. He became obsessed with her. He did seem to be infatuated with Katrina. Tim got really excited at having an opportunity to paint Katrina again. He had an obsessive desire for the Circassian. It's an obsession. An infatuation. A love. A desire for Katrina, a model!

Today Tim took the day off. Today he had spent the day relaxing. He sat by the fire. The sybarite took comfort from luxury. He overindulged in sybaritism. He took the time to rest himself. He had a sybaritic tendency to indulge in luxury at leisure.

At noon, Katrina arrived at the studio. At the time of her arrival, Katrina had been punctual. Tim who had been waiting for her got up from his chair and welcomed the model.

Katrina wore a beautiful black dress, boots and pearls.

Tim pointed to the chair. Katrina sat down on the chair. The leggy model looked graceful. The artist standing at the easel began to paint Katrina. The Circassian was stunning, her elegance lady-like. The model sitting struck an attitude. The Artist painted an elegant model. The Artist worked according to the model's requirements which were a modern natural look. Her expression was radiant. Her countenance naturally girlish. Her nature childlike of sweet innocence. The Artist concentrated on painting the model. The model was effective and a natural professional.

Finally, the Artist completed the portrait after the model's two sittings.

The Artist appeared to be satisfied with his work. The Artist hoped the Model approve of it. Katrina gave her approval. Katrina was pleased and satisfied with it. A satisfied customer.

The Artist gained satisfaction from painting a model. (The Artist had an obsessive interest in models since modelling was their passion.)

It was rewarding and satisfying. He enjoyed the experience.

Tomorrow, Katrina would come and pick up her portrait from the studio. This portrait of hers was an obsessive possession. Katrina was obsessed with exhibitions and photography.

Chapter 7:
The Discussion

That afternoon Tim waited for Katrina to arrive. Katrina arrived at the building. Katrina entered the studio. As Katrina came in, Tim welcomed her. Tim handed Katrina a bubble-wrapped portrait.

Katrina took it. Appreciating the thoughtful Artist.

"Is there anything else I can do?" asked Tim.

"I would like you to paint me. A portrait picture, picture. Anything," responded Katrina.

"When do you want me to begin? Can we talk about it? Let's sit down," pointed Tim.

Simultaneously Tim and Katrina sat down on a chair each. They both relaxed in the studio. They sat opposite each other. From lack of space, they could not move because of claustrophobia. Everywhere else in the studio remained claustrophobic with bubble-wrapped paintings and pictures put against the wall. There were also equipment and accessories for photography as well as lighting.

"Shall we discuss it?"

"Let's do. I require you to paint me a portrait of me in my garden. The background could be the climber roses. Can you do that?"

"That is romantic," exclaimed Tim sweetly.

"When can you begin? I want it done," prompted Katrina.

With enthusiasm, the Artist agreed to undertake the work. To paint Katrina.

"I would love to. I can start next week."

"I will call you. To discuss it."

Tim tapped his fingers on the chair. "Please do."

The Artist ogled the photogenic model. (He had previously seen Katrina's portfolio. He had admired her photographic image. The model's childlike innocence and purity. He seemed to think of her as being puritanical.

They both got up. They shook hands.

Katrina left the studio. The attractive model was picked up by her friend in a car parked in the street.

Tim was pleased with having met Katrina again. He hoped to see Katrina again. He did wonder if there would be another next time. Would this be the very last time he would ever see Katrina again?

The next day Tim rang Katrina. They both had a telephone conversation. A very short discussion. They both arranged to meet up. The Artist kept to the arrangement. Tim was scheduled to paint Katrina at her home in a very lovely garden. The Artist was fascinated by Katrina who was a millionairess and jet-setter.

During the afternoon at Katrina's house, the Artist

came. Agreeing to the arrangement. In the garden, Katrina stood still near the beautiful climber roses on the trellis all over the wall. The Artist stood by his easel. The Artist painted the sexy, curvaceous model for about two hours before eventually leaving to go home.

The Artist returned again the next day to finish off the picture. When the professional Artist had finally finished the picture, the model with a thrill looked at it with great interest and curiosity. Katrina greatly admired it. Katrina approved of it. Giving her necessary approval which Katrina expressed,

"I love it. It's lovely. It's just great," exclaimed Katrina.

The Artist felt satisfied. He did like her nice agreeable remarks of approval.

Leaving the detached house, taking his things, he put them at the back of the van. He closed the van door. He got in his van to go home. Katrina stood outside the house in the drive watching the Artist go.

The model desired to be painted again and again.

On another day, Tim delivered Katrina's picture. Katrina appreciated the delivery.

Katrina was so happy and pleased with it.

Tim left to go back to his studio to work. Tim desired Katrina. The Artist desired romance. A (romantic) relationship!

Chapter 8:
The Garden Picture of Katrina

The Artist kept his agreed arrangement. He went to Katrina's house in preparation for his session of painting. There he put up an easel and sorted out the paints he would use. The Artist painted a garden scene of the model standing and holding a rose. The scenery of a country garden. The Artist painted the model. Katrina looked placid, nonchalant and cool in her natural pose. The model stood still on the lawn gracefully and held in her hand a short-stemmed white rose. Katrina wore a lovely white dress, gold jewellery and canvas shoes. The imagery symbolised a virginal (married) woman.

The Artist was irritated at her moving. He insisted on professionalism from the model.

"Keep still. Don't move. Don't twirl the rose," cautioned Artist.

As a result, the model stood still and stopped twirling the rose. Katrina obeyed the Artist. In obedience to his order. After the first session, they completed the first sitting.

The Painter came back the next day to Katrina's house to finish off the picture. The garden scenery of a woman standing while holding a rose. The Artist completed the second session and final sitting.

After completion, Katrina was delighted and pleased with it.

In joyous appreciation, Katrina kissed the Artist who stood still admiring his work. To their surprise, they both ended up kissing each other. In their moment of passion. Their kiss was passionate.

The next afternoon the Artist came to Katrina's house to deliver the bubble-wrapped, framed picture. Tearing the bubble wrap from the picture, the satisfied model approved of the picture. It was another model's approval!

Chapter 9:
The Picture of a Field
(A Model's Pose)

On a hot day, Tim and Katrina went out along the fields. Somewhere there out in the fields the Artist painted Katrina lying down in a field of daffodils. Katrina raised a daffodil to her nose and smelled it. Her poise was beautifully graceful. Her pose a natural one. The model had grace and elegance. The Artist painted the model quickly. He hadn't time to come back there to engage in another sitting for the completion of the picture for a second session. The Artist was a perfectionist and seemed to be discontented and dissatisfied with it. Nonetheless, the Artist painted well. He did a good picture.

About an hour later they both took a break. They had a picnic lunch out in the lovely fields. A romantic picnic.

Katrina took out a tablecloth from a wicker basket. Katrina lay a tablecloth on the field. Katrina took out a big lunch box which contained sandwiches, two bottles of lager and fresh fruits. They sat down near a tree. A shadier spot away from the direct sunshine. They both ate a picnic and relaxed together. The Artist felt happier at being alone with Katrina a model. He had never ever felt as beatific and blissful as this before. Katrina appeared to be happy at being alone together with an Artist. It was her motive and intention to be with an Artist. Her objective was to be painted regardless of her circumstances.

"Was it love?" asked Tim.

"It was love," replied Katrina.

"Are you happy with my work?"

"Oh. Yes. I am pleased."

"Anything else you want me to do?" asked Artist.

"Not at the moment."

After the picnic Katrina cleared up and put everything away neatly in the wicker basket.

At present, the Artist resumed painting the model posing in the fields with her natural grace. The gorgeous model was elegant and graceful. Her girlish looks sultry. Her make-up was beautifully applied to her features. Thus, making her look quite beautiful.

The Artist rushed his picture. He finished completing it in another hour. He felt exhausted, tired and fatigued. He had been lethargic and lackadaisical too.

Katrina got up from the ground. Going towards the easel. The curious model in wonder took a look at the painted canvas. Katrina admired the picture. Katrina approved of it.

"I love it. It's great!" exclaimed Katrina joyously.

The Artist accepted the model's approval of it. The Artist seemed to be quite happy and pleased with the model's remarks of approval. The Artist felt quite contented and satisfied with it. He looked at the canvas. The sublime picture of a model in the fields. A summer paradise picture.

Driving Katrina home, Tim spent the night at Katrina's luxury home. It was an artist and model relationship!

Chapter 10:
Tim's Last Personal Delivery

A few days later, Tim delivered a picture to Katrina's house. Katrina took the bubble-wrapped picture and thanked him. The provocative model then shocked the Artist.

"Please go! My Husband will be back soon. I can't see you anymore. That's how it is. It won't work out between us."

Tim was disappointed at Katrina's rejection. He knew this would be the last time he would ever see Katrina. Katrina's shock had upset him. Tim in disgust stormed out of Katrina's house.

Tim arrived home feeling very upset and unhappy. He rested in the armchair in the Lounge.

His Mother burst in. The concerned Mother saw her son's unhappy expression.

"Son. What's wrong? Why are you down?"

"I have had a disappointment. A model won't see me again."

"Son. Get on with your work. I tell you the model is not worth it. Keep on painting," urged Mother.

Tim stayed indoors. He still felt disappointed. He

had been attached to Katrina. He loved her. He had fallen in love with her!

Tim felt utter misery. He was deeply unhappy and miserable. He stayed in his bedroom for hours.

The next day he went to the studio. At the studio, Tim took down the portrait of Katrina. He put the unwanted portrait with some of the other paintings and portraits which were not valuable and remained unsold.

On a day off Tim went to an Art Gallery. At an exhibition there, he saw various Artists' works. Tim marvelled and admired all of the Artists' works. Tim had a great interest in these Artists and Painters. The Artist had a passion for Art.

Leaving the Art Gallery in a rush, he felt inspired. His inspiration was thrilling. He had joyful satisfaction. He hoped to paint another model quite soon. (He thought of the next time he painted another one. It was a desire and fantasy of his!) If he could first overcome being too upset, disappointed and dejected. All because of the model's rejection and deep shock!

Chapter 11:
The Sitting

During the afternoon a model entered the studio. The Artist welcomed the model attending her modelling session to do her sitting.

The Artist painted the natural blonde. Her fairness was rather beautiful. The Artist painted a portrait of the blonde model. The professional model struck an attitude.

Her childish and girlish expression was happy, the model's look on her face radiant. From the sun her golden blondeness was so beautiful. Her thick, silky long hair tumbled down, all the way down to her back, her gold hair curly with ringlets and plaits.

In two sittings the Artist finally completed the portrait. The Artist was pleased with his work. The experienced model favoured the Artist. Requesting more work and assignments in the near future.

The Artist had been cautious as he had suffered a bad experience recently with a temperamental model. Working, the Artist had good conduct. He looked forward to working with Gabriella again. The tall model of Italian descent.

Coming home late that night, Tim went to bed late. He dreamt about last night!

At a gathering at a house, Tim met models and photographers. Tim being invited had still felt vulnerable and exposed. He mixed with photographers, Artists, jet-set and fashion models.

There to his surprise, he met Gabriella from Milan with other models. At that time the gorgeous models seemed to be far more interested in photographers than anything else. Losing interest in the Artists they spent more of their time with professional photographers. Gabriella was vivacious, frivolous, amiable and polite. For a while, Gabriella spoke briefly to the Artist. Since photographers and personnel from a top Modelling Agency required her to go with them at once. Demanding her attention.

Tim wondered what was happening. He had been distracted by the Host who attracted attention. Tim appeared to be confident, cheerful and despondent.

He met Gabriella unexpectedly. He was overwhelmed at meeting her. He had not expected this encounter. He seemed surprised to find that Gabriella had been invited. Attending her invitation. Gabriella remained unapproachable to everybody else.

The model's unapproachableness was her characteristic!

Leaving the do sooner, Tim had been disappointed. He drove home. Would he give up being an Artist? Tim would proceed with other things. Regarding painting, he was obsessed with painting. It was an obsession of his. Seriously he would now start to paint something else. The Artist was losing interest in painting models. He was becoming unenthusiastic, apathetic and uninterested in painting models and beauties.

He now wanted a change of course to everything. Of course, a better prospect in Art.

Chapter 12:
The Artist's Triumph

An Art Dealer came to Tim's house. He invited him over to take a look at his work. The Art (collector) Dealer looked at his oil paintings and pictures. They were wildlife, still life, nature pictures, landscapes, seascapes, nocturne, monochrome, abstract and reproductions.

The Art Dealer standing had looked at them. Losing interest and desire to look at them. Tim's friend seemed uninterested in all of them. The Art Dealer unconsidered them for his Art Collection.

"Where are they all?" enquired the Art Dealer.

The Artist answered his question.

"The best ones are in my family's possession," answered Artist.

"Er! Is there not one?"

Going around the house from room to room, the Art Dealer looked at every painting, picture and contemporaries. At that present time, nothing really interested the Art Dealer. His passion for Art was contemporaries, abstraction and Renaissance. A speciality of the professional Art Dealer. The Art Collector, Dealer had an obsessional interest in landscapes particularly and certain Artists' paintings and works. The Dealer, Collector took no interest in any of them. They were ordinary pictures, paintings and portraiture. Entering the Lounge the Art Dealer lost enthusiasm for looking at any others. The Art Collector was unenthusiastic and half-hearted at looking around further. He was knowledgeable about Art. He wanted to go and leave much sooner. The Artist tried to keep his attention by attracting him. The Artist tried to be attentive to him.

"Take a look at these ones," demanded Tim.

Tim took a portrait and picture stacked up against a cardboard box in a corner of a room. Tim handed it to the Art Dealer so he could look at them. A portrait of a model and a picture of a female figure lying in a daffodil field.

"I like it. It has acquired taste. Can I take them? I'll see what I can do with them. I can't promise you anything," said the Art Dealer.

The Artist agreed for the Art Collector, Dealer to take them. He didn't have an afterthought. Tim showed the Art Dealer out of the front door. Tim was pleased with the Art Dealer who took them.

A few days later Tim received a telephone call from his friend the Art Dealer. His company would commission the Artist to paint.

Tim rejoiced. Feeling overjoyed and triumphant at last. He clenched his fist in triumph at the good recommendation from the Art Dealer as well as from his Art Companies in London and New York.

One night Mother and son stayed up and took a look at the paintings on the wall.

"Which one do you like?" asked Mother.

The son preferred a brilliant colourful painting. SUMMER MEADOW. A beautiful landscape. Of a meadow scene. It still remained his favourite one.

"I really like that one. It's my favourite one," pointed son. "Which ones do you like?"

The aesthete pointed at her admirable favourites. These ones were a painting of a barn and a farmyard. Natural scenery of a farm and its land and summer scenery of a farmhouse on acres of ground.

"I do like them. They are lovely oil paintings," remarked son.

"How about that one?" pointed Mother.

Tim walked to a pretty picture. A contemporary on the other side of the wall. This one was a picture of an elegant Englishwoman smelling a rose out in the garden. Standing close to beautiful climber roses on a trellis on a stone wall in the background. The delightful picture was enchanting. A charm!

"I do love that. It's pretty natural. That one. I wish I could paint like that," exclaimed Tim expressly.

With wonder, the Mother thought.

"Aren't the models to your liking?"

"Oh! They are. My pictures and portraits could be so much better," commented son.

Son and Mother walked somewhere else in the house. They had seen another portrait somewhere there. This one was of a beautiful natural blonde. The Artist liked this one for sentimental reasons and purposes. He preferred this one. It was one of his favourite portraits. This European woman was a foreigner. This lovely model, Continental and Mediterranean.

With deep natural love, the Artist had a deep affection for the blonde model.

"I do like this one very much. It means an awful lot to me. It is pretty sentimental to me. I love it! I love her too!" pointed son.

They both ended their time together by looking at the contemporaries. None of these really interested the Artist. Making no particular difference to his Art Collection. They were hanging on the wall in preference to all the other ones. They were reproduction paintings.

Chapter 13:
The Artist's Last Moment (With the Company of a Model)

Tim was invited to a get-together. He attended a get-together. There at a country house, he met guests. These invited guests were the jet set, Photographers, Artists, Models and Personnel. At the get-together, Tim met interesting people, guests. He had the same interests in common with them. He spoke to a few Artists.

They were successful at working for top Art Companies. (The Artists' works on exhibition at Art Galleries and Libraries.)

One of them he spoke to was freelance. His works were an international success. Tim avoided the photographers on purpose. He thought of them as being manipulative panderers who exploited models. He observed them, not knowing much about them. What he did know about them though was that they may be connoisseurs. Actually a few of them. One of them he took notice of in his observation was a Fashion Photographer for a woman's magazine. He envied how Professional Photographers had good relationships with models. Most relationships between them were nonexistent. He felt embarrassed by his personal failures. His embarrassing relationships with models. He knew his time with them would come to an end. It was a bitter disappointment.

Someone came around with a tray of drinks in a crowded room which felt claustrophobic. It was full of guests as they socialised altogether. Tim took a glass of sparkling aperitif. He gulped it down. Tim mixed with guests around the room as they chatted amongst themselves in groups. Wearing a tuxedo, Tim felt rejected at being shunned and ignored by everybody else. He took discomfort from being uncomfortable. As a few guests spoke to him. Greeting him by his name. He called out to them. He had no wish to impress any of them. He acknowledged each of them by smiling back at them. One of them was a charmer. Tim wished he hadn't come here. He was having an unhappy time here. Tim wanted to leave to go home. He didn't want to give an impression of being unsociable. Their lack of interest disinterested him.

Going out of the crowded room, Tim went elsewhere. He was relieved to get out of the crowded room. He wandered down the hall, looking at paintings there. He rather liked them. He saw antiques and luxury décor. He smelled leather. It was reminiscent of deluxe cars.

He walked past guests. No one paid any attention to him whatsoever. Walking around the country house Tim felt lonely. Again, he had been spurned, shunned and rejected by everyone. He got a sense of purpose at being given an invitation to the get-together. He still felt unwanted and unloved. Nevertheless, he still appreciated his invitation. The light now was becoming darker and darker outside. A dark summer night.

Tim came out into the garden. At present, there were fewer and fewer guests out in the garden: twosome, threesome and foursome present at this time of night.

Down at the bottom of the garden, he saw Gabriella all alone. Tim was surprised to see her. He met her unexpectedly. The stunner in a sequined evening dress looked stunning. She wore stilettos and was adorned with jewellery. The Artist was utterly surprised at the sight of her alone.

"Gabriella. It's you! What are you doing here?"

The unembarrassed model smiled at the Artist.

"I must go. My Papa is waiting for me."

The Artist swooned at the model. He was stunned by her beauty. The model was engaging, her sweet charm delightful. He felt surprised at meeting the model unexpectedly.

"Will we see each other?" asked Artist.

"I am going back to Italy," replied Gabriella.

The Artist was overwhelmed with shock. He appeared to be emotionally upset, sad and tearful.

"Are you. So soon."

With appreciative love, the model touched the Artist. Gabriella had a deep appreciation for his thoughtfulness.

"Thanks for painting me. Yeah! Good of you," smiled Gabriella.

"Thank you. It was a pleasure."

"It was great."

Both Artist and model embraced each other. An emotional passionate embrace and farewell between them.

Quickly Gabriella walked off ahead in the direction of the country house. Reaching indoors, Gabriella entered the house. Walking through the house, she stopped by the front door. There, at the front door, Gabriella expected to meet her Papa waiting for her. Her chauffeur drove them both home.

Tim was very sad that Gabriella had gone. He had no wish to stay there any longer. Without giving any explanation for his departure to anybody, he quickly left the house. In the drive, he got into his car which was parked in reserved parking. He drove home.

As Tim got home, his Mother stayed up, waiting for her son to come home. Tim came in. He sat in an armchair. Tim yawned. He felt tired and sleepy. He was deeply sad and tearful. The Mother saw her son's sad expression. He suppressed his tears.

"Son, what's wrong?" asked Mother.

"Nothing, Mom," replied Son.

"Son, you can tell me."

Tim pictured it in his mind. He imagined it. "Tonight, I saw the woman of my dreams. Now she's gone away. I will never see her again," said Son sadly.

The sympathetic Mother expressed her expressive sentiment.

"Don't take it to heart, Son. Don't give your heart away. Don't get attached. Don't let your heart break. Don't be sad! Don't get heartbroken. You will love again, I assure you. Now is not the time. Do not have any regrets."

The Mother kissed her son goodnight. The concerned Mother had a deep concern for her son. The parent left her son alone downstairs to reflect on Gabriella.

Tim was too sad. He deeply missed Gabriella whom he deeply loved and remained fond of. He desperately wanted to see Gabriella again!

With such desire, the Artist was deeply attached to the model!

Tim remained slumped in the armchair. He sat still in a position of discomfort. He could not overcome the disappointment and deep sadness he felt towards Gabriella. The love he desired. It broke his heart!

Chapter 14:
The Request for Painting

Jess and Mrs Stewart came to see Tim at his Mother's house. They were good friends of theirs. While Mrs Stewart spoke to Tim's Mother, Tim took the opportunity to talk to Jess alone in another room. Tim and Jess privately talked together alone in a reception room. They both preferred to have their privacy without intrusion.

Jess pressed for an answer. "Will you paint me?" She paused. "Well, will you?"

Tim responded. His response was immediate. "Oh! Of course, I will paint you. You're a priority," replied Tim.

Jess sat down on the settee. She put her hands on her hips gracefully. Expressing her desirability.

"Hey! Don't you think I am sexy? You ought to paint me," insisted Jess.

"Why don't you get yourself photographed?" said Tim advisedly.

Without having any doubt of being painted, Jess still remained confident.

"I can do that as well. That would really please me. I do think I am right for it. Don't you? To be painted."

"Of course, you are. How about tomorrow? At noon at the studio."

Jess acknowledged her confirmation.

"I will be there."

"Do be ready for 12 p.m.," insisted Tim.

"Who is the woman? In the picture?" wondered Jess.

"Why?"

"She's a natural. It's such a nice picture. I like it," remarked Jess.

"Oh. That's a model. My Mother met her one day. She agreed to be painted. I like that one."

With curiosity, Jess wondered,

"Do you know all of the females?" asked Jess.

"I don't know them personally," denied Tim.

"Oh! C'mon! You must know them," expostulated Jess.

"I do and I don't. If you know what I mean. Mine is a fiery relationship," added Tim.

"Huh! It is. Is it?" smirked Jess.

"You're easy-going. You'll be fine with me. I am an Artist," reassured Tim.

"You are. Are you? I shan't be a problem," assured Jess.

Jess got up as her Mother called out to her Daughter.

"Please, excuse me. I must get going. It's time to leave," said Jess impatiently.

Tim undesired Jess. He thought Jess had a bad personality. A temperamental redhead!

Within less than a quarter of an hour, Jess and her bitchy Mother left the house. Both welcomed. They had outstayed their welcome.

On Thursday at noon, the Artist beautifully painted Jess. A handsome woman. It took about two sittings for the Artist to complete the portrait with such fine consummation.

When finally finished Jess took a look admiringly at the portrait. Jess approved of it. Her approval of it was satisfying. Jess looked at it in admiration. Jess had self-love for herself. An obsessive narcissism. Jess was obsessed with it! Jess was pleased and satisfied with it.

A few days later Jess's Mother, Mrs Stewart, collected the framed portrait from the studio. Mrs Stewart personally thanked the Artist. A good friend of his Mother!

Chapter 15:
The Artist's Last Resort to Paint

Tim would go to family friends' houses. There he saw various pictures, paintings and portraits. A few of them were either dilettantes or aesthetes. Most of the others were probably casual about Art itself. They were either knowledgeable or ignorant about it.

Tim acquired talent over the years from his painting. He was dedicated, committed and disciplined in his work. He had a passion for Art.

He was ignorant about some Artists and Painters. He remained knowledgeable about famous Artists and Contemporary Artists. He revered and admired them. Actually, having great admiration for famous Artists. Their masterpieces! He was fully aware of various Artists and Painters. Their works and collections. Also, as well as one in particular. One Artist's tragic life!

Their Artworks were vulgar or avant-garde. Their (aesthetics) aestheticism in Art a uniqueness. The Artists' marvellous works.

Tim, an Artist, unexplained the Arts as he remained coy about them.

Next time he would be better prepared for it. He had knowledge about it as well as being ignorant about other Artists. He learned more about Art in a positive fashion.

The Artist still remained desirous, dissatisfied and discontented with himself. He still wanted to accomplish and achieve more success.

Regarding models, he felt ambivalent and non-committal towards them. Some of them at least. Ultimately the Artist would give up painting models and therefore do other things which were more productive, wiser and sensible. He used his common sense concerning them. Also lacking love for them all. Feeling depressed, dejected and despondent and unhappy at times. He had hatred and resentment for the models, certain ones in particular. He would not discuss how he felt about them. He kept it private and confidential.

One day Tim received a phone call, an unexpected surprise. It was from Gabriella. An Italian model. Gabriella was coming to the UK to do modelling. A photo shoot. Gabriella was feeling desirous and wanted to be painted. Gabriella negotiated in accordance with the Artist's terms and conditions. The pleased Artist agreed to it. He painted another portrait and picture of Gabriella. This one was a dreamy daydreamer smelling a rose in a beautiful garden. These particular ones were commissioned to the ecstatic delight of the triumphant Artist. The happy Artist gained self-esteem, pride, dignity and success and wealth. He felt much happier now. At last!

He had dreamt of this moment. His dream came true!

He never did court Gabriella. It wasn't possible

under the circumstances. However, Tim was triumphant despite Gabriella's refusal to meet up with him for a date.

Chapter 16:
The Artist's Times Alone with Nature

A few months later Tim spent days at home in his garden. There he painted garden scenery. A garden scene of the radiant sun shining. The natural sunlight. It's glorious radiant sun rays. He captured the great natural beauty. Its natural glory! The Artist's pictures included painting pictures of a sunset, sunrise and afterglow. His vivid imagination was sublime and glorious.

Alone with nature, Tim took delight and wonder at it. He felt much calmer, peaceful, happier and relaxed at being alone. (Not having the burden from nature. His constant resentment for them!)

During those days along with nature and its glory there, the Artist painted some good pictures. He used pastels and watercolours. He also did a watercolour which was well done.

The Artist appeared to be discontented and dissatisfied with them. He aimed for perfection. As he was a perfectionist. However, he felt satisfied with having achieved his main objective. Looking back, he remembered that summertime with such joy. Realising there would never be times like these ever again!

The Last (rose) picture

Gabriella, a model having a great appreciation for the Artist, allowed herself to be painted. The Model agreed to the arrangement, on the understanding that it was her last and final one. On a lovely sunny day, the Artist painted the natural Model. Standing with a background of rose bushes. Gabriella, dressed in a lovely white dress held a white rose to her nose. She smelled the scent of a beautiful white rose. A natural pure white rose. It symbolised the female's purity and innocence. Her expression was nonchalant and naturally beatific. Her sweet look of girlish innocence. The Artist captured the essence of the model's natural pose. The nature of her beatitude. Capturing its breathtaking glory. The actual natural look and glory.

The picture remained one of the Artist's least favourite pictures. (A pretention. A pretentious Model.)

As a perfectionist, he remained dissatisfied and discontented with it. The Artist kept calm and cool. He grumbled at having to rush doing this picture. (Only in the allocated time of fewer than two sittings.)

The natural Model approved of the Artist's picture. Gabriella was satisfied with it. The professional model gave her approval of it. The picture, "White Purity", was a satisfactory work of Art. Using oil paints, the Professional Artist created a virginal beauty with a natural look. Quite stunning.

The Artist Times Alone with Nature

Spending time alone Tim would paint landscapes. (The Artist had lost the desire to paint Females now as this infuriated him. His obsessive desire for them was a fantasy!)

At these times alone, the Artist preferred not to have a strained relationship with any models!

Day after day, Tim Gardener would paint landscapes or garden scenery. He gained inspiration from the beauty of nature. This interested and fascinated him as he was a good painter. He was inspired by nature. It was a wonderful fascination!

He took pleasure in painting. It gave him great satisfaction, pleasure and enjoyment. As weeks passed by, he spent more time outside in the garden and countryside rather than in the studio. Working in a studio made him feel claustrophobic and moody. Every day he gained a sense of inspiration from having the freedom to paint in the natural environment. It was an agoraphobic environmental thrill and joy at working outside in a warm climate. The sunny beauty of it was an inspirational joy as well as a motivational incentive to paint such natural scenery. Particularly of natural landscapes. Every day the Artist painted something new and different from his previous works. He was fascinated by nature. An aesthete, the Artist acquired perfection in his art and work. His inspiration was a motivation.

- THE END -

*Available worldwide from
Amazon and all good bookstores*

www.mtp.agency

www.facebook.com/mtp.agency

@mtp_agency